introducing

KYLA MAY

miss.behaves

written & illustrated by

kyla may

PSS!
PRICE STERN SLOAN

♡

this Book is dedicated to
my amazing Mum, who inspires
me to Dream & be myself.

♡

Copyright © 2005 by Kyla May Pty Ltd. All rights reserved. Published by Price Stern Sloan, a division of Penguin Young Readers Group, 345 Hudson Street, New York, New York 10014. PSS! is a registered trademark of Penguin Group (USA) Inc. Printed in China.

Library of Congress Cataloging-in-Publication Data

May, Kyla.
 Introducing Kyla May Miss.Behaves / by Kyla May.
    p. cm.
 Summary: Kyla May writes in her journal about her life, her family, and her many daydreams, which repeatedly get her in trouble at the Melbourne, Australia creative arts school she attends.
 ISBN 0-8431-1370-7 (pbk.) — ISBN 0-8431-1457-6 (hardcover)
 (1. Imagination—Fiction. 2. Schools—Fiction. 3. Diaries—Fiction. 4. Australia—Fiction.) I. Title: Introducing Kyla May Miss Behaves. II. Title: Introducing Kyla May misbehaves. III. Title.

PZ7.M4535ln 2005
(Fic)—dc22
                                                                            2004015201

          ISBN 0-8431-1370-7 (pbk)   10 9
          ISBN 0-8431-1457-6 (hc)   10 9 8 7 6 5 4 3 2 1

HI, MY NAME IS KYLA MAY!!

I am __11__ years old & i live in AUSTRALIA......& i have a very, very active *imagination*.

Mum gave me this journal last week after i got detention 4 daydreaming in class (like, can i help it if music class makes me imagine i'm a Pop-Star ???) Anyway, she hopes this JOURNAL will B a good place 4 me 2 'channel my energies' — whatever that means?

2 B honest i do have a bad habit of daydreaming...one minute i'm concentrating...the next minute i'm someONE else, someWHERE else...lost in my *imagination*. (it's totally cool!) ☺

'Cause i'm always in ☹ TROUBLE, my school friends call me: Miss. Behaves. ♥

← very active imagination

C my special dictionary @ back of journal

yes, yes... my excuse!

this is ME!

3

A bit about 'ME: ♥ ♥ ♡ ♥ ♡ ♥ ♥ ♥ ♡ ♥ ♥ ♥

i'm from Melbourne, the 2nd largest city in
Australia (& the coolest place in the world!) ✳

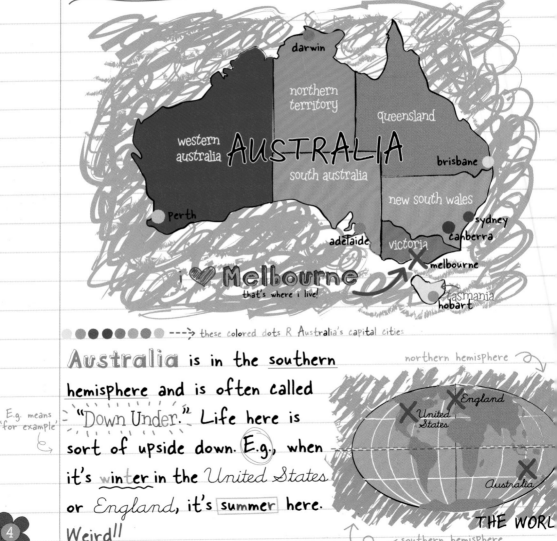

darwin

northern
territory

queensland

western
australia AUSTRALIA
south australia

brisbane

new south wales

perth

sydney
canberra

adelaide victoria

melbourne

i ♥ Melbourne
that's where i live!

tasmania
hobart

● ● ● ● ● ● ● ● ● ---> these colored dots R Australia's capital cities

Australia is in the southern
hemisphere and is often called
"Down Under." Life here is

E.g. means
'for example'

sort of upside down. E.g., when
it's winter in the United States
or England, it's summer here.
Weird!!

northern hemisphere

England
United
States

Australia

THE WORL

southern hemisphere

4

i totally LOOOOOVE where i live. The beach is right down the end of my street. Every day i walk 2 the beach with MY absolutely gorgeous doggie, Fifi-belle.

our secret spot amongst the rocks

miki's house (my best friend!)

the Pier

the bike track

my street

the beach

my house

the park

'@' means 'at'

Hidden @ the far end of the beach is our 'special secret spot' that NO ONE else knows about. (so shhhh? don't tell anyone!) There, Fifi & i tell each other our secrets & problems — Fifi-belle is a brilliant listener. Sometimes i also write in my journal as Fifi collects shells — Our 'special secret spot' is our most FAVORITE place EVER 2 'hang out.'

these are some of Fifi's most treasured shells

In **Australia** we say some words differently...E.g.:

'G'day' = Hello   'Aussie' = Australian
'Bush' = the Countryside   'Crikey!' = Wow!
'Dag' = Nerd   'Fair dinkum' = Real, Genuine
'Lollies' = Sweets, Candy   'Mate' = Buddy, Friend
'Mozzie' = Mosquito   'No worries!' = Okay!

Australia has the most adorable unique animals in the whole wide world. Some of my favorite animals R Wombats Koalas & Kangaroos.
Soooo cute!

a koala!
btw, koalas live in trees & eat GUM leaves

a wombat   btw, wombats live in holes

ME as a joey in my kangaroo mummy's pouch!

Hmmm...sometimes i *imagine* what it would B like as a baby kangaroo (also called a 'joey') living in the snuggly warmth of my mummy's pouch. Joeys live in there from the time they're born...until 8 months old. How cool would that B....???

this is the pouch

btw, kangaroos don't walk - they hop!

6

Australia is V. multi-cultural, which means people have IMMIGRATED here from loads of different countries. Some of my best friends R Russian, Italian, Greek, Chinese & English. As a result, typical Aussie food is a variety of dishes from all over the world. However, our most traditional meal is a barbeque (BBQ)...followed by a yummy dessert made of meringue, called Pavlova...YUM!!!

Mum, Dad & i go 2 the beach most weekends, where i swim. Dad is teaching me how 2 SURF. Cool, dude! Hmmm...imagine if i were a world champion Surfer...? ☺

this is called a 'tube'

When Dad is busy working, Mum & i go shopping. We LOVE shopping, as do most girly girls — it must B in our genes! We never, ever get tired of shopping. Unfortunately Dad does when he C's the credit card bill! (hee hee!)

Speaking of Mum & Dad, i better introduce them 2 U...

This is **Mum**

This is my family:

This is **Dad**

This is *Mum's* art. i don't really understand what it's a picture of??? It's called "Abstract Art." "Weird Art." if U ask me!

This is our house, which **Dad** designed.

And of course this is **Fifi-BELLE**

i love our house, as do all my friends...they R all very jealous of how modern & funky it is. It's almost like a "space-age" house.

My MUM's name is Star May. She's an artist, a painter in fact. She's really successful...4 an artist. i've been told that heaps of artists struggle financially, like have no money! Mum says she'd B an artist even if she wasn't successful 'cause it's her obsession, her calling in life, her vocation.

(hmmm....whatever that means??)

she's TOTALLY unique

Please note the chopsticks in Mum's hair. Who ever heard of that??? Dad says Mum's "arty." She sure doesn't dress like anyone else's Mum! Mum likes 2 dress in Spanish, Indian & African styles, depending on her mood...(which, i assure U, changes regularly). i tease her about it, but actually it's pretty cool.

My DAD's name is Jackson May. He is an architect; he designs modern houses. Dad's sort of successful, but he struggles every now & then. Being an architect is a challenging job 'cause his "clients" never have enough money 2 afford his "space-age" ideas. Dad always seems frustrated.

Mum & Dad R both "creative." They use their imaginations 4 their work. i reckon that's why i have an extra BIG imagination. 'Cause they R creative, they totally encourage me 2 use my imagination...but only @ the RIGHT TIME!

Introducing my (non-human) best friend: **Fifi-belle**.

♡ ♡ ♡

She's a French Poodle. Most people think poodles R snobs, but i swear, Fifi-belle isn't!

yes, i am!

fifi-belle - 4 months old

Soooooooooo CUTE!!!!!

This is my FAVE photo of Fifi-belle as a puppy (ohhh, she's totally cute). Mum & Dad gave her 2 me 3 yrs ago. She's been completely by my side, through my highs & lows. (highs = not getting in2 trouble, which is rare) (lows = getting in2 trouble). She knows me totally better than anyone else in the world. She's my soul mate. I looove her sooooooooo much. Like, i can't imagine life without her

the bonapartes

Hello, my name is Mademoiselle Fifi-belle Bonaparte III. Daughter of French Poodle World Champions, Madame and Monsieur Bonaparte. I am a tenth generation champion Poodle. My ancestors were the royal pets of King Louis XVI of France.

Mademoiselle Kyla is not just my owner but also my soul mate. We are two of a kind. We love to shop, dress up and spend time at the beach.

Mademoiselle Kyla May caters to my every obsessive need. I am always lavished with delicious doggie treats and my bedding is made of the highest quality silk and down feathers...just as royalty deserves! Mademoiselle Kyla spoils me rotten. I couldn't imagine life without her.

i'm her bestest friend, not miki!

This is **Miki Minski**. We've been absolute bestest friend since we were like 6 years old. Oh, except 4 the time we had a **fight**!

As i remember...i was @ Miki's house & we were pretending w were 2 princesses, sisters in fact, ruling our royal kingdom Possibly i got a little 2 carried away with royal jealousy & accused Miki of being a traitor.

...i then had her BEHEADED!!!! (...oops!) ☹

12

Regrettably, i ignored her 4 ages (an entire ½ an hour!),
'cause as I explained 2 her then, without a head, a person
can't talk. Hmmm...unfortunately Miki did not appreciate
my sense of humor!

Luckily our horrible
"misunderstanding"
finally ended after
i begggggged &
grovellllllllled 4
forgiveness nonstop.
(Sometimes Miki
is sooooooooooo
sensitive!)

a photo
Mum took,
just before
i had Miki
beheaded!

hmmm...do i look prettier?

Princess Kyla May and
Princess Miki Minski

Miki & i play after school most days, except of course
when i (accidentally) get in trouble & have detention.

13

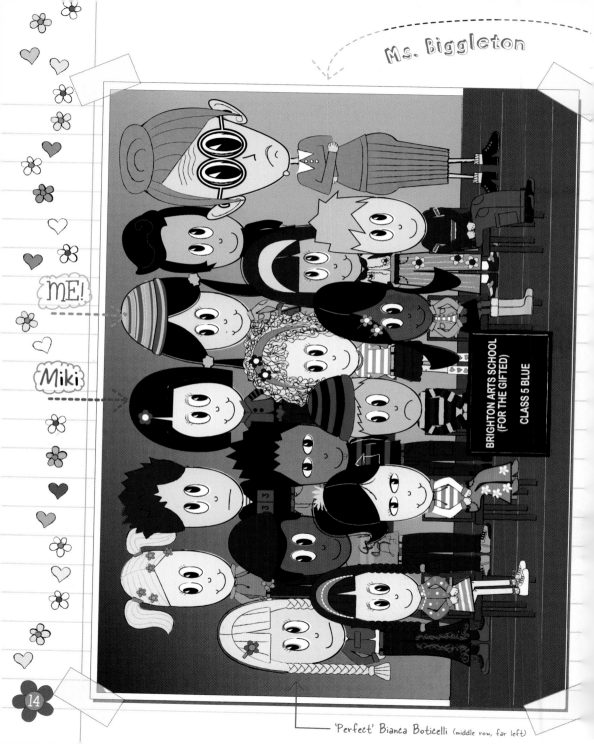

Ms. Biggleton

ME!

Miki

BRIGHTON ARTS SCHOOL
(FOR THE GIFTED)
CLASS 5 BLUE

'Perfect' Bianca Boticelli (middle row, far left)

Here is my school photo: ✿ ♥ ✿ ✿ ♡ ✿

Check me & Miki out! (top row)

My school is a totally cool 'Arts School.' ✿
Everyone is extra, extra <u>talented</u> in creative subjects
♥ (E.g., art, dancing, drama & music). ✿ ☺

Unfortunately with <u>extra talent</u>, people can B <u>extra</u>
annoying. Some R major DRAMA QUEENS (& kings),
especially 'Perfect' Bianca Boticelli!

This is Ms. Biggleton. My homeroom, **Math**
& GEOGRAPHY teacher.

don't worry... familiar!

She ALWAYS catches me daydreaming & then gives me
detention. (In case U R not completely familiar with
detention, it's when your unforgiving, impatient teacher
keeps U after school & gives U <u>unfair punishment</u>.)

Check out my punishment!!!!! P.T.O. ↰ ☹

(please turn over)

15

I must always concentrate in class

I must always concentrate in class

I must always concentrate in class

I must always concentrate in class

I must always concentrate in class

I must always concentrate in class

I must always concentrate in class

I must always concentrate in class

I must always concentrate in class

I must always concentrate in class

I must always concentrate in class

I must always concentrate in class

I must always concentrate in class

I must always concentrate in class

Usually i loooooose concentration during math class.
And that's 'cause Ms. Biggleton is possibly the most
booooooring teacher ever. I swear, it's the only time I get
distracted! Usually,
I love class!
Here is a picture of
Ms. Biggleton...
Hmmm...
Does she totally remind
U of something?
Mmmm...
Like, possibly a...bug?!!??

Hmmm... yes! she does.

EXHIBIT B: ↗
a BUG

EXHIBIT A: ↗
a photo i took of BUG-EYE
without her realizing!

We actually prefer 2 call Ms. Biggleton: BUG-EYE. Her
huge eyes & her skinny legs & arms totally suggest...INSECT.
Even her clothes kinda smell of moth balls & she sort of
makes a funny buzzing sound as she hovers over U.

17

BUG-EYE can B soooooooooo annoying.

Hmmm...sometimes i'm reaaaal naughty
& i *imagine* her...

but MayB snails R my fave insect. R they an insect?

...flying, buzzzzzzzzzzzing around...

...bugging me & my friends @ school...

19

Oh no...i forgot 2 mention this b4, but it's Friday's **Math** class now! Bug-eye is rambling on in her usual booooooring banter. The weekend seems soooooooo far away. ZZZZZZ ZZZZZZ How lucky am i that she hasn't caught me writing in my *journal*. (hee, hee, hee!)

Actually, i'm not the only one absolutely boooored 2 tears...E-V-E-R-Y-O-N-E IS! ......Even 'Miss. Perfect Teacher's Pet' – Bianca Boticelli.

Check it out...she's reading a fashion magazine under her desk! Bianca completely believes she's a **Supermodel!!!!** Hah, like WHAT A JOKE!
....i'd B such a better **Supermodel** compared 2 her!

Mmmm...can't U just C me as a famous **Supermodel?!**

...i'd live in PARIS, France — which is in Europe. PARIS is like the most *romantic* city in the entire world & the world's major Fashion Capital! (Hey...& the origin of French Poodles!)

...*imagine* ME being a gorgeous CATWALK MODEL?
(which means i'd wear designer clothes while walking along
a catwalk)

French flag

1950s vintage
pillar-box hat
with veil

ME as a SUPERMODEL,
living in <u>Paris, France</u>
...in designer clothes!

very
famous
Paris
street
where
models
strut
their
stuff

Avenue des Champs-Elysees

The Eiffel Tower,
Paris's most famous
landmark

striped
long-sleeve
tee

1950s
inspired
silk &
sequin
bag

silky cargo
pants
with silk rosettes
& fringed
with sequins

funky
silky
trainers

streets in
Paris
R so old,
they R
cobblestoned

wonder
what the
new brown"
is?

i'd strut my stuff @ the latest *Spring Fashion Parade*,
where the "new look" is street-fashion with a touch of
1950s glam & "brown is the new black," which apparently
means brown is the most popular dark color.

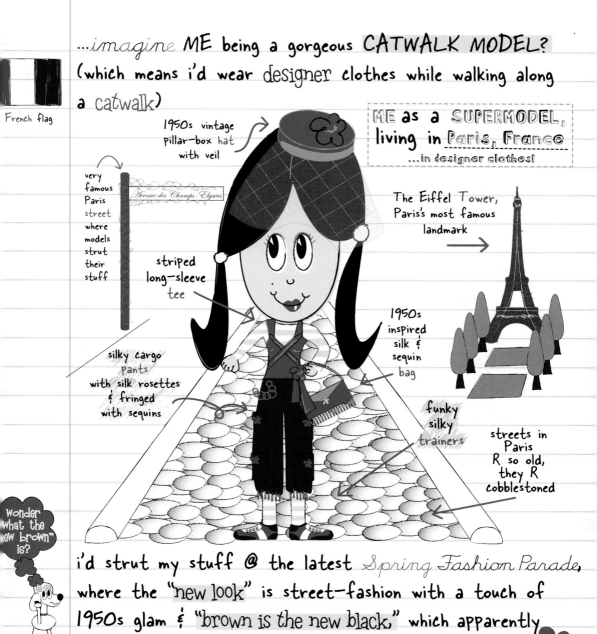

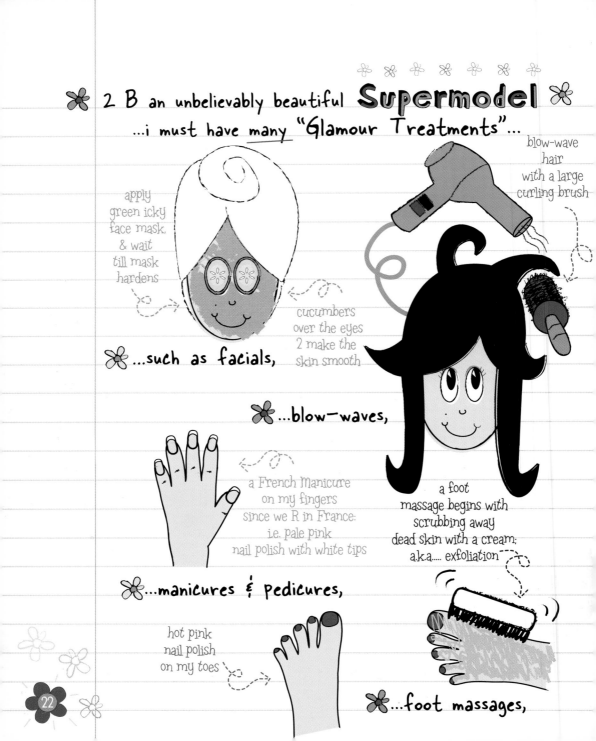

2 B an unbelievably beautiful **Supermodel**
...i must have many <u>many</u> "Glamour Treatments"...

apply green icky face mask. & wait till mask hardens

blow-wave hair with a large curling brush

🌸 ...such as facials,

cucumbers over the eyes 2 make the skin smooth

🌸 ...blow-waves,

a French Manicure on my fingers since we R in France: i.e. pale pink nail polish with white tips

a foot massage begins with scrubbing away dead skin with a cream; a.k.a..... exfoliation

🌸 ...manicures & pedicures,

hot pink nail polish on my toes

🌸 ...foot massages,

❀ ...mud baths,

hmmm...the things
i must do 2 B beautiful!
a mud bath refreshes
the skin all over

*supermodel
bathes here*

phew...make
sure U don't
stay in
the steam
bath 2 long!

❀ ...seaweed wraps

seaweed wraps R good 4
your skin!

❀ ...& steam baths.

i don't
need any
beauty
assistance...
m beautiful
enough!

❀ ...Oh la la! (which is French for Yeah!)
i'm soooo ready 2 B a supermodel.
"Glamour Treatment" 4 one, please?
❀ ...Bring it on!!!

(Hey, Fifi-belle could have equivalent doggie-beauty-
treatments! Hmmm...she already loves playing in mud.)

'Cause i'm living in France, i should know some French word

English: ## French:

"Hello"   =   "Bonjour" (i'll say as i glide IN designer clothing boutiques)

"Goodbye"   =   "Au Revoir" (i'll say as i stroll OUT of boutiques with designer outfits piled high)

"Hi"   =   "Salut" (i'll say 2 my bestest friends, who R all famous fashion designers, models & photographers)

"Yes"   =   "Oui" (i'll say 2 my millions, hmmm, ok, thousands of fans who request my autograph)

"Please"   =   "s'il vous plaît" (i'll say 2 my "Personal trainer" as i b 4 permission 2 eat crème caramel – a amazing French dessert, so yummy!)

"No"   =   "Non" (is what my "Personal trainer" will say about crème caramel, since supermodels must B in good shape...ohh like imagine not having desserts!!!! – I can't?)

"Thank you" =   "Merci" (i'll say 2 all the gorgeous French boys who buy me flowers)

"Sorry"   =   "Pardon" (Better learn this word, as i say it more than any other word in English!)

But absolutely most importantly:

"May i have a hot chocolate?"   =   "Je voudrais un chocolat chaud?"   (After all, when one is in France, one MUST have a hot chocolate... or 2...or 3!)

KM

Dioré

CHANNELE

Kylamay

Bonjour

24

Another thing 2 know is what 2 carry in my handbag (designer, of course!) as i travel around (hmmm...most probably in a limousine): *please note that everything is pink*

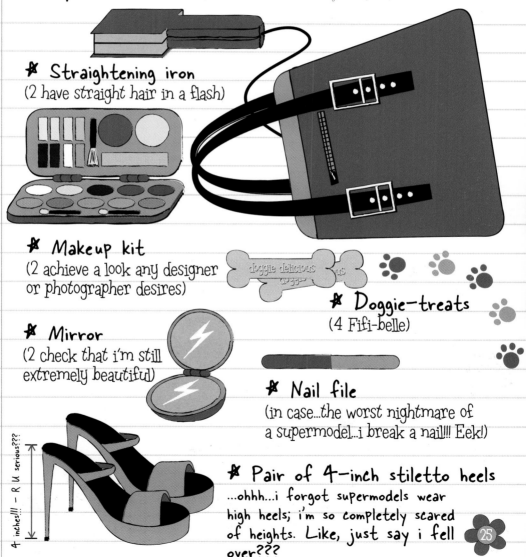

✱ **Straightening iron**
(2 have straight hair in a flash)

✱ **Makeup kit**
(2 achieve a look any designer or photographer desires)

doggie delicious doggie...us

✱ **Doggie-treats**
(4 Fifi-belle)

✱ **Mirror**
(2 check that i'm still extremely beautiful)

✱ **Nail file**
(in case...the worst nightmare of a supermodel..i break a nail!!! Eek!)

4 inches!!! – R U serious???

✱ **Pair of 4-inch stiletto heels**
...ohhh...i forgot supermodels wear high heels; i'm so completely scared of heights. Like, just say i fell over???

Not sure i want 2 B a **Supermodel** anymore!
Just imagine walking along the catwalk & (oh NO!) falling
head over heels in2 the audience!!!! Ahhhh...the
shame...the embarrassment!!!!

But then again, i'd travel the world 2 beautiful locations...

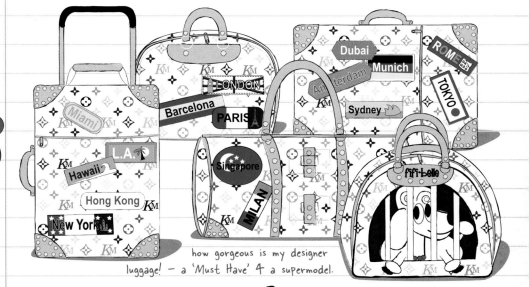

I love my travel case... leather of course!

Dubai
Munich
ROME
Amsterdam
LONDON
TOKYO
Barcelona
PARIS
Sydney
Miami
L.A.
Singapore
Hawaii
fifi-belle
Hong Kong
MILAN
New York

how gorgeous is my designer
luggage! – a 'Must Have' 4 a supermodel.

...wearing amazing clothes. MayB i could gradually learn
how 2 walk in stiletto heels? MayB there's an after-school
course i could do?

Speaking of school... **Oh NOOOOOOO!!!!**
  Sacre Bleu! (which is French 4 'Oh Dear!')........

eeek!!! this is not good.

"KYLA MAY!

ARE YOU PAYING ATTENTION???

PLEASE TELL THE CLASS WHAT THE ANSWER TO PROBLEM 4 iS?"

Arhhhh...hmmm...well, it's like...

Oh no...i'm TOTALLY in TROUBLE now!

Possibly the worstest (is that a word? Hmmmm, mayB not) WORST trouble i've been in 2 date.

28

i hate it when that happens!!!

...The whole class looks @ me as i stare blankly back @ BUG-EYE. My face burns bright red with embarrassment...

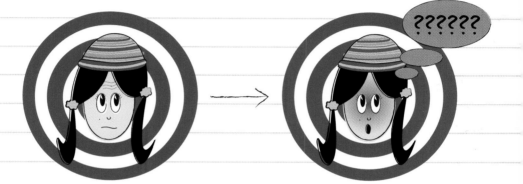

...My brain searches 4 an answer?????????????????????????? ????????????????????????? But nothing comes 2 mind. Nothing comes out of my mouth...

...BUT plenty comes out of BUG-EYE's!

"I'VE HAD ENOUGH OF YOUR DAYDREAMING.

GO TO THE PRINCIPAL'S OFFICE IMMEDIATELY!"

Here i am sitting outside the Principal's office...awaiting my punishment.

Our Principal is a lot nicer than BUG-EYE. But being sent 2 her office doesn't usually bring out the best in her personality!

i can't *imagine* this punishment is going 2 B enjoyable @ all. What could it B???? Hmmm...like mayB she'll make me her SLAVE 4 life!

NOW   YEARS LATER

many years later: nothing has changed, except of course, my age!

ball & chain: used commonly for preventing slaves from escaping

Or...mayB she'll send me 2 JAIL on a deserted ISLAND & i'll never, ever B able 2 leave?...i'll B all alone...except...

...4 ONE MILLION rats that will share my cell! Yukkkkk!!!!!!!
Oh, how i'd miss Fifi-belle soooo much.

Hmmm...mayB i'll blame BUG-EYE 4 my daydreaming 'cause she's like so boring? Every other ~~teacher~~ @ this school is interesting & i rarely daydream in their classes...oh, except that time in _geography_ when i thought i was Climbing Mt. Everest! Oh...& also that time in _drama_ when i thought i was a Hollywood Movie Star...oh, & in _painting_ when i thought i was a **World-famous Artist**, oh...& last week in _music_ when i thought i was a Pop-Star!

But, apart from that, i totally blame BUG-EYE! In my other classes i only sometimes daydream, but in _math_ i always do...there4 it's completely her fault! She is full-on boooooooooooring.

31

MayB what BUG-EYE needs is a (major) extreme makeover Then she'll B more interesting & i will NO LONGER get in2 TROUBLE.

BEFORE

Ms. Biggleton's Extreme Makeover!

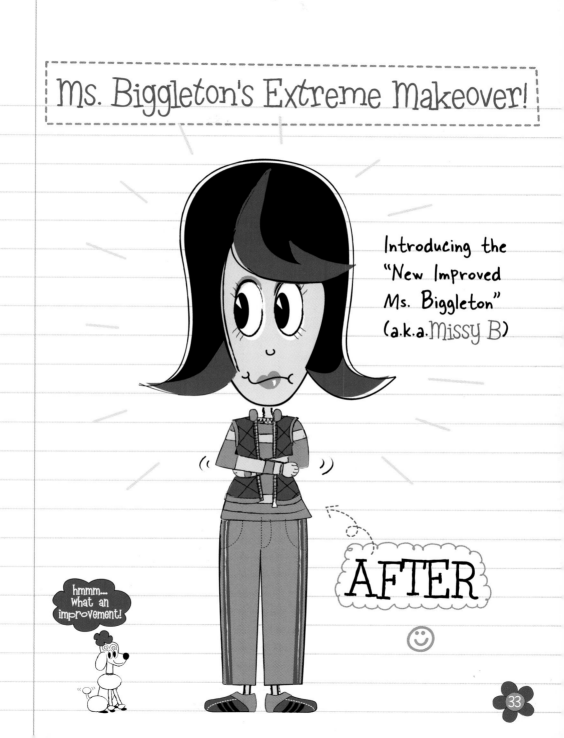

Introducing the "New Improved Ms. Biggleton" (a.k.a. Missy B)

AFTER

hmmm... what an improvement!

☺

Finally the *Principal* has decided my punishment:
instead of participating in **Ballet class**, which is NOW
(the last class of the day)...i must sweep the gymnasium!

So not fair 'cause
Ballet is my
absolute FAVE
class in the entire
world! & a brilliant
way 2 finish the
school week.

...Well, if everyone else is going to practice **Ballet**... ☺
then i can, 2!

Hmmmm...

Mmmmm...

hmmm?

Imagine being a famous **Ballet Dancer** in Swan Lake
(a.k.a. Principal Dancer), *the most wonderful ballet ever!*
...i'm wearing a beautiful feathered tutu...&...hmmm...

Or imagine being a DANCER in a music video.
Hey, i could B on MTV! Yeah!!!

...Hmmm, what about a professional dancer in a
"Broadway" MUSICAL? "Broadway" is a street
in "Times Square" in New York where major
full-on famous musical theaters R located. ♫ ♪

↓

BROADWAY

Broadway street sign

"Times Square" is where all these totally **huge** flashing lights & billboard posters R. Mum & Dad take me 2 New York heaps. (Unfortunately i have 2 leave Fifi-belle @ home with Nana. But Nana always spoils Fifi with treats.)

i adore New York, it's like, completely exciting. It's where the absolute BEST hot dogs in the world come from. i swear. (But don't worry, Fifi-belle, they're not real dogs!)

i'm not stupid! Know what a hot dog is! YUM!

Mum always tells me how inspiring New York is 4 artists. Her paintings R exhibited in a studio in "SoHo," which is somewhere in "downtown" NYC. (btw: NYC = nickname 4 New York City)

famous NYC skyline

Dad can't get enough of the architecture in NYC. The city's jam-packed with amazing buildings, some old, some new. It's a city of skyscrapers (which R really, really tall buildings). There R heaps of famous buildings in NYC, such as the Empire State Building, the Chrysler Building, the Flatiron Building & the Guggenheim. (heard of 'em?)

Wow, just imagine being in New York right now...

37

New York's amazing skyline

Mum in one of her Spanish outfits

I ♥ NY

Me eating the best hot dog in the world ...sooo delicious!

Ballet class is over & so is the school week.....well 4 some! (not me, yet!)

Miki & my 2nd best friend, Sienna Longmore, just invited me 2 Sienna's house 4 a sleepover. (Possibly out of charity, Bianca Boticelli is invited 2.......Bianca drives me BALLISTIC.) She is V. annoying, always showing off about her perfect clothes, her perfect horse & her perfect hair...blah, blah, blah...perfect, perfect perfect...)

& her 'perfect' horse! (wish i had a horse)

Perfect Bianca

& her 'perfect' designer wardrobe — most of which comes from Europe...how outrageous! (& perfect!)

i totally looooove **sleepovers** – MUM even gave me the absolute cutest new pj's that she had Fifi-belle's Photo printed on. They R awesome. The other girls would B so so so JEALOUS!!!

i said i may B able 2 come after Detention, but who knows how long BUG-EYE will keep me back???

My new Fifi-belle sleep set

eye-mask

sleeping beauty

Pj's

How cute R my pj's!!!! Mum even got Fifi-belle a bed & eye-mask 2 match.

slippers

Ohhh, i bet they'll have **loads** of cakes & sweets.

& guaranteed they will do makeovers on one another – Sienna has heaps of fantabulous **makeup**... Oh! & mayB they'll do a fashion show...i'm so good @ modeling & fashion coordinating.

i can't believe the FUN they will have WITHOUT ME!

i've finished the sweeping & NOW the Principal has asked
me 2 write an essay in front of BUG-EYE
(wasn't sweeping enough???)
My essay topic is:
   "Why is Math so important to my education?"
Pleeeeease, what am i supposed 2 write???
(There's NO WAY i'll B leaving here b4 dark.)

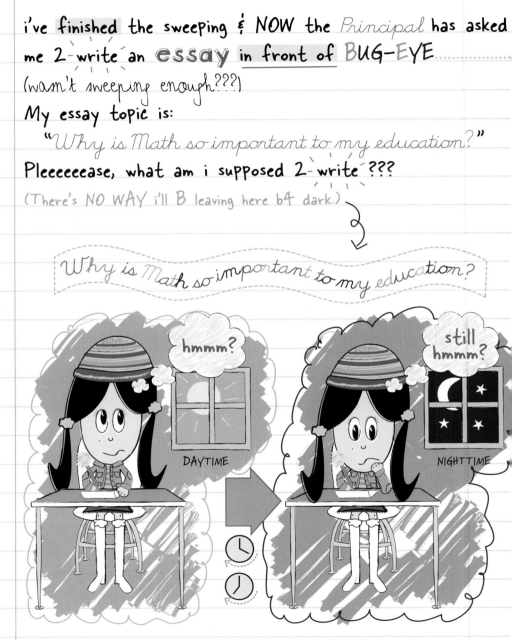

Why is Math so important to my education?

hmmm?

DAYTIME

still hmmm?

NIGHTTIME

Oh no, i just realized that Mum & Dad R going 2B so furious. Like, they'll never let me go 2 Sienna's now. 😞

they never get upset with me!

usually this is the zone Mum & Dad hit

Mum and Dad understanding

Mum and Dad happy

it's not 2 often the gauge gets 2 here!!! Only on special occasions.

Mum and Dad upset

MUM & DAD TOLERANCE-O-METER

Hmmm...but then again, they R usually sort of understanding. MayB they'll just make me miss out on the yummy food & games, but AS IF they'd make me miss out on the actual sleepover? (not that we sleep!) – oh dear, this could B devastating!

@ sleepovers, i am ALWAYS the last person 2 stay awake...& i always tell the scariest stories. Like really, how can they have a sleepover party WITHOUT me – i AM the party! Oh, this is totally miserable. 😞 😞 43

????

i'm finding it so difficult 2 concentrate on this essay all i can think about is what the girls R up 2. It's even more irritating that Bianca is there!...& not ME!!!!!!!!!!

Hmmm...MayB Bianca will take MY spot...& become Miki & Sienna's BeSTeST friend?

Kyla May can be in my secret club any day

...MayB Bianca will start a **secret club**... & ban ME from membership. (i knew i couldn't trust Bianca!)

MayB THEY will make special **bracelets**?...

...Perhaps THEY will make up a club 'dance routine'

...& mayB THEY will design a **secret alphabet** so THEY can write one another letters that only THEY will B able 2 understand?

A B C D E F G H I J K L M

N O P Q R S U V W X Y Z

If i had a secret club, this would be MY secret code: (But don't tell Bianca Boticelli!)

@ least i'll still have Fifi-belle...i wonder what she's doing now?

Could she possibly B having fun WITHOUT ME? MayB she' totally *depressed* 'cause i'm not with her?

teddy not snuggled

slipper not delivered

dinner not eaten

dinner

cricket ball not fetched

tissues

chew rope not chewed

squeaky toy not squeaked

Yeah... Yippee... shopping for ME!

MayB Mum has taken her shopping 2 cheer her up? Fifi-belle looooves getting new outfits! (just like me!)

Mmmm...i wonder what she'd get? Possibly the gorgeous cowgirl one we saw @ the mall the other day...
...& i could get an outfit 2 match!

cowgirl KYLA MAY

co-starring FIFI-Belle

What about a **kimono**?

But seriously, AS IF i'll B getting any new outfits! Have i forgotten that i'm in detention?

Princesses of the Far East:
KYLA MAY
& FIFI-BELLE

Hmmmmmmmmmm..."Why is Math so important to my education?"...

my best friend

Hmmm...as if Miki would join a secret club **without me!** She is my best friend. We completely understand each other. & we have soooo much fun together.

Our absolute FAVE imaginary game is **MS. GALAXY !!!!** The best game ever in the whole universe. (Miki & i made it up, in case U haven't heard of it.) It's sort of like Miss. World & Miss. Universe Beauty Pageants, but totally better. After all, it's the whole Galaxy. Which means creatures from other planets can compete. (But sorry, Fifi-belle, no dogs!)

The Sun

Mercury

Venus

our moon

Earth
(where i come from
of course!)

Mars

Jupiter

Saturn

Uranus

Neptune

Pl

i am
very beautiful
AND
very clever

Miki & i *imagine* we're contestants in the "Final 10." O these 10, the judges choose the winner (1st) & runner-up (2nd). Ohhhh...i really hope i WIN!!! (Please cross your fingers 4 m

The final event is the "Talent" contest, where we perform our best talent (obviously)! It's important 2 B clever, as well as beautiful, since *looks aren't everything.*

My "Talent" is Ballet (like, of course, no surprise there)!

i dance majestically. The crowd applauds & yells "Encore, Encore!!!" They R dazzled by my performance.

Then...complete silence, (shhhhh...) the crowd hushes in anticipation...everyone's anxious 2 know who the winner is?

Fifi-belle can't even look, her paws R trembling... who will the judges crown MS. GALAXY ?...

49

MEEEEEEEEEEEEE!!!!!!!

(of course, i mean who else did U think would win!)

Sometimes i play this game on my own. However, Ms. Mars often comes really close 2 snatching 1st place. She's my greatest threat.

She is very beautiful, in a Mars kinda way. (That is, she's RED, like really sunburned! But she's actually not, that's the color of people from Mars.)

Mars
(a.k.a. The Red Planet)

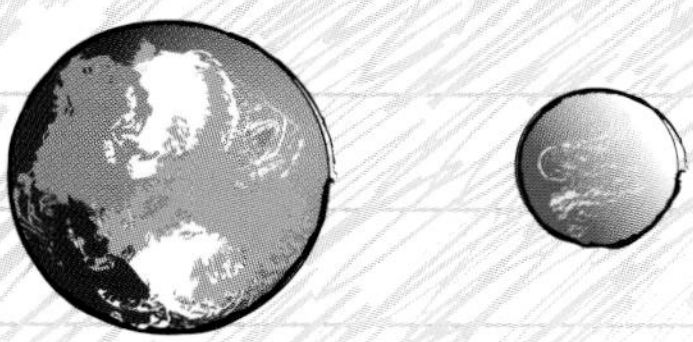

Mars is the closest planet to Earth

Ms. Mars

Her "Talent" is juggling comets, which is pretty impressive... believe me!

Once i win MS. GALAXY, *imagine* how my life will totally change when i'm an INTERNATIONAL...

...actually UNIVERSAL...

no...GALACTIC CELEBRITY?!

Imagine MY face (& Fifi-belle's) on the covers of magazine

Even every boy (& alien) wants 2 marry me... after all, i'm the most talked about girl in the Galaxy.

With all the glamour comes some hard work. As a representative 4 the Galaxy, i must travel 2 poor planets & feed helpless, starving 'beings'...

But *back* 2 the GLAMOUR!!!...imagine all the gala events i'll B invited 2? Heads will (turn) as i... MS. GALAXY, make my Grand Entrance.......

Very Important People only
(that's ME!!!)

VIPs only

what do you mean MOST!?!

i'll B photographed on the "red carpet." Like, wherever the party is...i'll B there (...lookin' stunning...of course!)

(Fifi-belle will B almost as famous AS ME,...sharing my spotlight.)

Also, my role as **MS. GALAXY** would mean...

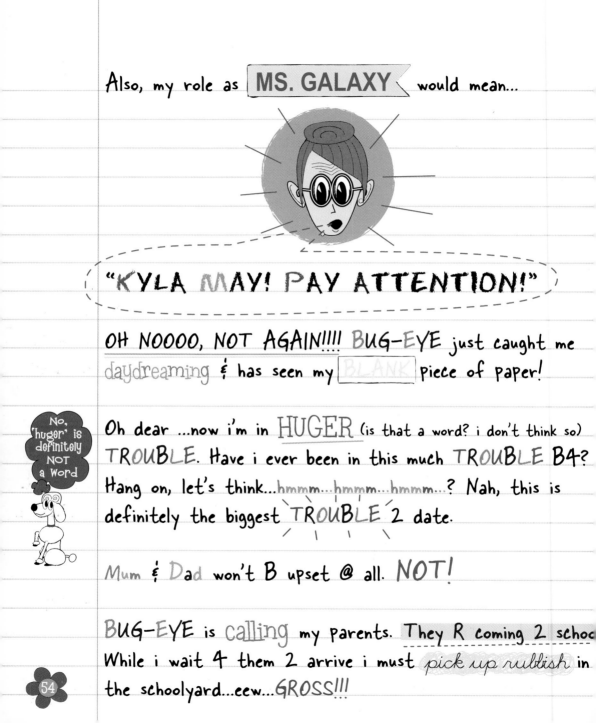

"KYLA MAY! PAY ATTENTION!"

OH NOOOO, NOT AGAIN!!!! BUG-EYE just caught me daydreaming & has seen my BLANK piece of paper!

No, 'huger' is definitely NOT a word

Oh dear ...now i'm in HUGER (is that a word? i don't think so) TROUBLE. Have i ever been in this much TROUBLE B4? Hang on, let's think...hmmm...hmmm...hmmm....? Nah, this is definitely the biggest TROUBLE 2 date.

Mum & Dad won't B upset @ all. NOT!

BUG-EYE is calling my parents. They R coming 2 schoo While i wait 4 them 2 arrive i must pick up rubbish in the schoolyard...eew...GROSS!!!

Look @ what i must pick up: GROSS!!

moldy uneaten sandwiches   banana skins   apple cores

This is equivalent 2 "child labor"...surely this kind of punishment is totally illegal? If not, there should definitely B some law against it.

Imagine if i were a POLITICIAN...i'd completely put a stop 2 it. (Since Politicians R the people who make up & change laws) Hmmm...imagine the POWER i'd have?

What other laws could i change?

* Dogs can go 2 school with their owners.
* i can drive a hot pink sports car even though I'm only 11.
* Manicuring & Pedicuring will B compulsory school subjects.
* Every school field trip will B overseas. We'll stay in 5-star hotels and spend lots of money.
* Bianca Boticelli will B my personal assistant, starting each day by cleaning my room.

In fact, being a Politician could B utterly fantabulous.

Oh dear...doom & gloom ahead!!! Dad just arrived @ school
BUG-EYE is talking 2 him.
Dad looks V. worried.

What will Mum & Dad do 2 me?
MayB they will sell ME?

Or send ME 2 strange Aunt
Gladys's sheep farm in the
Australian outback,
where there R heaps of SNAKES
& SPIDERS? Major scary stuff.

FOR SALE

Baaaa

Baaaa

scary
spiders &
snakes
somewhere
here!!

Hmmm...MayB **Fifi-belle**
& i could run away & live on
the beach, camping out @our
'special secret spot'?

But i could NEVER leave Mum & Dad, ☹ i love them 2 much, & they love me...

...speaking of Mum...why didn't she come 2 school with Dad? i'm sure BUG-EYE said Mum & Dad were both coming??

Well, that wasn't 2 bad @ all. i sooooo thought i was in major TROUBLE. Instead, BUG-EYE told Dad that she can relate 2 my overactive imagination; she used 2 have the same problem when she was a child.

She wants 2 support my creative imagination, but also help me concentrate harder in classes where i don't use my imagination as much, such as **Math**.

BUG-EYE thinks that i don't have enough CREATIVE outlets 2 express myself. There4 she has suggested i do extra art classes, & these classes will give me extra credit!!! (Can U believe it? Like, is this the same teacher? Or have i misread BUG-EYE all along?)

✳ i am totally shocked — BUG-EYE, i mean Ms. Biggleton, actually understands me!!! ☺

Oh no...just when i thought everything was going so well...
Dad told me WHY Mum didn't come 2 school.

Fifi-belle has gone missing!!!!!

LOST

French Poodle called 'Fifi-belle'
HUGE REWARD if found

Mum & Dad believe she's gone in search 4 ME 'cause i
was kept back @ school so much _later_ than usual.

Oh, poor Fifi-belle...she must B sooooo scared.

Where could she B????????

Please...i hope nothing bad has happened?

Firstly Mum thought Fifi-belle was hiding in our house, so she searched everywhere.

.... But NO Fifi!

Then she searched the street & asked our neighbors 2 look in their houses.

But, NO LUCK...no one has found her!!

Mum & Dad have asked me 2 really "think" as 2 where Fifi-belle could B?

Hmmm...let's think...like, if i were Fifi-belle where wou i go? Imagine i'm scared and looking 4 me?

Hmmm...possibly 2 my school? No, 'cause i would have seen her when i was picking up the rubbish.

MayB she has gone 2 Miki's house?

Or the mall?

Nah, she knows not 2 ever, ever cross the road. She would never B that naughty, & i reckon she's already totally frightened, the cars would scare her even more.

If i were Fifi-belle, i'd go somewhere 2 feel real safe......& somewhere where i may B?

Hmmm...think, KYLA MAY, think...? Use your brain.. like, where would i go if i were Fifi-belle???????..

☆ Ohhhh...i know, i know, i know!!!!!!!! ☆

i'd go 2 our 'special secret spot' on the beach!...

Yeahhhhhh! i am soooooooooo happy!!!
...Fifi-belle was @ the beach!

☺☺☺☺☺☺☺☺☺☺☺☺☺☺☺☺

She was shivering when we found her, but her little tail wouldn't stop wagging. She licked up all my tears ...& Mum's 2.

i'm sooooo happy

Mum & Dad R so proud of ME. @ last i've used my brain & my imagination @ the RIGHT time. Cool! (Hey, i reckon i could B a spy when i grow up – i'm such an awesome detective.)

62

AND....U'd never ever guess what Mum & Dad have decided?!...i can GO 2 Sienna's sleepover... AND i can take Fifi-belle with me — double cool!

oh no.....Sienna's Mum accidentally cut off Bianca's face in this photo....how upsetting....NOT!

btw. the girls looooooved my 'fifi-belle' pj's

The girls were SO excited 2 C me...they even waited 4 my arrival B4 they ate the yummy chocolate caramel cake with strawberry icing!

WHAT A DAY! ☺

KYLA MAY's Dictionary:

2	=	to/too
2day	=	today
4	=	for
4ever	=	forever
a.k.a.	=	also known as
B	=	be
B4	=	before
btw,	=	by the way
C	=	see
fantabulous	=	fantastic & fabulous added togeth
i	=	I
i.e.	=	that is
in2	=	into
mayB	=	maybe
P.T.O.	=	please turn over
R	=	are
U	=	you
V.	=	very
@	=	at
&	=	and
=	=	equals

i give U permission 2 use my dictionary with your friends!